HOGWOOD
Steps Out

HOWARD MANSFIELD

HOGWOOD
Steps Out

A Good, Good Pig Story

Illustrated by BARRY MOSER

A NEAL PORTER BOOK
ROARING BROOK PRESS
NEW YORK

Thanks to Dan Harper, especially, and Laurie York of York Kennels,
who allowed me to photograph her hogs in Conway, Massachusetts.—B.M.

Copyright © 2008 by Howard Mansfield

Illustrations copyright © 2008 by Barry Moser

A Neal Porter Book

Published by Roaring Brook Press

Roaring Brook Press is a division of Holtzbrinck Publishing Holdings Limited Partnership

175 Fifth Avenue, New York, New York 10010

Distributed in Canada by H. B. Fenn and Company, Ltd.

Library of Congress Cataloging-in-Publication Data

Mansfield, Howard.

Hogwood steps out / by Howard Mansfield ; illustrations by Barry Moser. — 1st ed.

p. cm.

"A Neal Porter book."

Summary: Hogwood the pig escapes from his pen and enjoys a spring day exploring neighborhood gardens.

ISBN-13: 978-1-59643-269-7

ISBN-10: 1-59643-269-1

[1. Pigs—Fiction. 2. Gardens—Fiction.] I. Moser, Barry, ill. II. Title.

PZ7.M3172Hog 2008

[E]—dc22

2007013199

Roaring Brook Press books are available for special promotions and premiums.

For details, contact: Director of Special Markets, Holtzbrinck Publishers.

Printed in China

First edition May 2008

Book design by Jennifer Browne

2   4   6   8   10   9   7   5   3   1

For Christopher Hogwood, barnyard maestro
—H.M.

and to
Ellie Chase Parsons
January 23, 2007
Sweet little Miss Number Nine
—B.M.

Mud. That's what I smell
this morning. It's rich, it's inviting. It's like
the smell of a cake baking in the oven.
I have been in my pigpen all winter. Cozy, but boring.
I was outside a few times, but my feet get cold in the
snow. They turn bright pink. We pigs have sensitive feet.

But this morning, it's all different. It smells different.
And sunlight is spilling in, warming me up.

Before I really know what I'm doing, I'm letting myself out. I know how to open my gate. Even though my feeders keep adding things to stop me, I watch and learn.

Pull that cord, and that cord. Rock the gate back and forth, back and forth, and—there! the gate is open.

Where to go? Ah, the ground is squishy, soft. And the breeze brings news . . . over that way someone has planted . . . lettuce. Let's go have a taste. Or maybe let's eat it all.

Oh, nice garden. All the soil is plowed. I could have done that for them. Now for a snack.

Who's this? The gardener is running toward me, waving his arms. Shouting. No need for that. I have big ears—I can hear him. I can also run right over him, but I won't.

I weigh six hundred pounds. I'm a lean six hundred pounds.

Once I was the runt of the litter. I was very sick and felt
bad. My brothers and sisters were twice my size. They thought
I wouldn't live.

But my feeders took me home in a shoe box. They fed me
and I got better. So I don't knock people over.

"GRrunnnt! GRrunnnt!" I growl out. That stops him. I run right toward him. He jumps. Then he dives to catch me, but I race away. "Christopher Hogwood!" he yells. He knows me. We have done this before. What can I say? He grows the sweetest squash. I like to think that he grows them for me.

I smell something else on the breeze. Deep, earthy. Vintage earth. Rich mud. I follow my nose.

On my way, I stop to check out a green lawn. I put my nose down, and it just rolls back. I can roll up a whole lawn like a carpet if I want. I tear a huge hole in this green lawn. Stick my snout far in. There's dirt all over my face. It feels good. Try it sometime.

A woman is running toward me. It's her lawn, I guess. I don't think she wants to thank me. The lawn does look better. Much improved. I'd like to roll in that dirt, but I'll move on.

A man in blue has joined the chase with the woman and the gardener. His car has a throbbing red light on top. "Hogwood! Hogwood!" they call. "And a good day to you, too," I grunt back.

I'm far ahead of them. I'm near the deep, deep earth smell. A big yellow thing is digging a deep trench. I'm impressed. I'll go offer my congratulations.

"Good work! Good work!" I bellow. The man inside the big yellow thing freezes. He stops digging, jumps down, and races away. Some people can't take a compliment.

I look down into the trench. You can always learn something new. Pick up some pointers. I'm happy to see this huge hog wallow.

The man in blue sneaks up on me and drops a rope around me. He starts pulling. I pull back. "GRrunnnt! GRrunnnt!"

I could pull him to the moon, but I'm ready to go home. I'd like a nap. After a while I let him lead me back.

"Christopher Hogwood," he says. "You have to stop rambling around." He, too, knows my name. He has taken me home many times. I have him well trained.

Walking back to my pen I recall that the gardener
has planted watermelons. And that the woman with
the lawn has planted pumpkins. The man in blue gives
me an apple to urge me along. I eat it and slow down.
I'll get a few more apples from him before I'm home,
and lie down to sleep in my soft bed of wood shavings
and cool earth. It's going to be a good summer.

God bless gardeners.